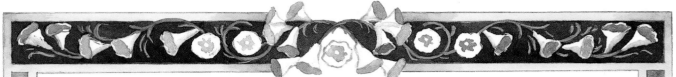

Once-Upon-A-Time

Three Tales of Enchantment

Sleeping Beauty

The Little Mermaid

Beauty and the Beast

Retold by Marilyn Helmer • Illustrated by Kasia Charko

Kids Can Press

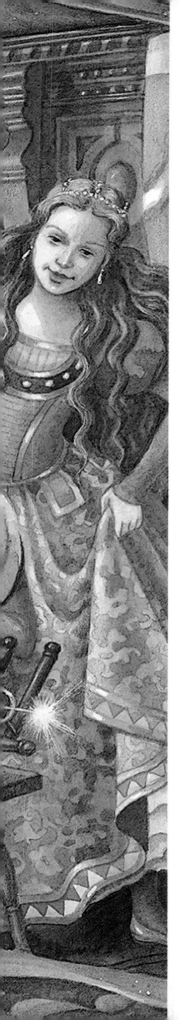

For Sandra and Tanya, two enchanting young women — may your lives always be happily ever after. — M. H.

To Thomas. — K. C.

Text © 2001 Marilyn Helmer
Illustrations © 2001 Kasia Charko

Kids Can Press acknowledges the support of the Ontario Arts Council, the Canada Council for the Arts and the Government of Canada, through the BPIDP, for our publishing activity.

Published in Canada by
Kids Can Press Ltd.
29 Birch Avenue
Toronto, ON M4V 1E2

Published in the U.S. by
Kids Can Press Ltd.
2250 Military Road
Tonawanda, NY 14150

The artwork in this book was rendered in watercolor.
The text is set in Berkeley.

Series Editor: Debbie Rogosin
Editor: David MacDonald
Design: Marie Bartholomew
Printed in Hong Kong by Wing King Tong Company Ltd.

This book is smyth sewn casebound.

CM 01 0 9 8 7 6 5 4 3 2 1

Canadian Cataloguing in Publication Data

Helmer, Marilyn
   Three tales of enchantment

(Once-upon-a-time)
Contents: Sleeping Beauty — The Little Mermaid — Beauty and the Beast.
ISBN 1-55074-843-2

1. Fairy tales. I. Charko, Kasia, 1949– . II. Title. III. Series: Helmer, Marilyn. Once-upon-a-time.

PS9565.E4594T465 2001   j398.2   C00-932861-0
PZ8.H3696Th 2001

Kids Can Press is a Nelvana company

Contents

Sleeping Beauty

Once upon a time there lived a King and Queen who longed for a child. When at last the Queen gave birth to a beautiful baby girl, it seemed that their happiness was complete. A splendid christening party was planned, and all the noblest families in the kingdom were invited.

"We must ask the twelve good fairies to be godmothers to our child," said the Queen.

"Indeed," said the King, "for they will give her gifts that no mortal can give."

On the day of the christening, a sumptuous banquet was prepared and tables were laid with the finest linen and silver. A special table was set for the good fairies. At each of the twelve places was a plate, a goblet and cutlery, all made of precious gold.

Soon coaches and carriages, each one grander than the one before, arrived in stately procession. Servants escorted the guests to the banquet hall, where the King and Queen sat waiting. Beside them the little Princess slept peacefully in her cradle.

Just as the festivities were about to begin, the sound of dainty footsteps came from the courtyard. A hush fell over the room. All eyes turned to the door as the twelve fairies entered. Then, unexpectedly, a thirteenth fairy appeared. She had not been invited because she was an evil fairy, known for her wile and wickedness.

The King and Queen gasped in dismay. Now that the wicked fairy had come, they dared not ask her to leave. The Queen quickly ordered a servant to set another place. Since there were only twelve gold dinner settings, the thirteenth place had to be laid with silver.

When the wicked fairy saw the others eating from gold dishes, she was furious. "First they fail to invite me," she hissed, "then they set my place with common silver. They'll pay dearly for this insult!"

The fairy who was sitting beside her heard everything. Certain that her wicked sister had an evil plan, this good fairy resolved to be last in line when it came time to give the Princess her gifts.

As soon as the banquet was over, the fairies came and stood by the royal cradle. One by one, they presented the Princess with such magical gifts as beauty, grace, wisdom and good nature. Soon she had every virtue a child could possess.

Then came the wicked fairy's turn. "My gift to you is a curse," she shrieked, glaring at the little Princess. "On your fifteenth birthday, you will prick your finger on a spindle and die!"

Everyone trembled at the terrible words. Now the last fairy stepped forward. She could not undo the curse, but she could soften it. "My gift to you is life," she said to the Princess. "You will prick your finger on a spindle, but you will not die. Instead you will sleep for one hundred years. Then you will be awakened by the kiss of a king's son."

That very day, by royal command, every spindle and spinning wheel in the kingdom was destroyed.

The Princess grew up to be a lovely young girl, endowed with all the gracious gifts the good fairies had given her. As for the wicked fairy's curse, there seemed no chance that it could come true.

On the morning of her fifteenth birthday, while everyone was busy preparing for the celebration, the Princess wandered through the castle by herself. At the end of a winding passage, she discovered a narrow stairway. The steps led her to a small door. Wondering what lay beyond, she pushed it open and looked in. Against the back wall stood an elaborate bed. Beside it sat an old woman, turning the wheel of a strange wooden object.

The Princess stared in surprise. "What are you doing?" she asked.

"I'm spinning thread," the old woman replied.

Curious, the Princess stepped forward and reached out to touch the wheel. The spindle whirred and, in a flash, the silver tip pricked her finger. At the same moment, the old woman disappeared with a triumphant shriek of laughter. But the Princess did not hear it, for in that instant she sank to the bed in an enchanted sleep.

Everything grew still. There was not a sound to be heard. A deep sleep fell upon every living creature within the castle walls—the King and Queen in the throne room, the cooks in the kitchen, the maids in the chambers, the horses in the stables, the dogs in the courtyard and the cat in mid-stretch. Even the flies on the wall stopped buzzing. The Princess herself lay as though she were in a dream.

In no time at all, a high hedge sprang up around the castle. Twisted trunks and thorny branches wound themselves together, forming a living wall that no one could penetrate. Nothing like it had ever been seen before. Word of the mysterious hedge spread throughout the land, and countless stories were told of the sleeping Princess. Young men came from near and far to see her, but the hedge held them back.

Time went by, and people forgot the castle was even there. Thus, for one hundred years, everything lay in an enchanted sleep until one day a Prince rode by. When he asked what lay beyond the hedge, an old man told him the legend of the beautiful sleeping Princess.

"I must see her for myself," said the Prince.

"That is impossible," the old man warned. "All who have tried to pass through the hedge have failed."

"I will not fail!" declared the Prince. He turned his horse toward the hedge. Magically the thorns changed into delicate flowers, and the hedge parted like a curtain to let him pass. When he reached the other side, the Prince found himself in front of a great castle. He quickly dismounted and went inside.

All was silent save for the echo of his footsteps as he moved through the marble halls. In room after dusty room, he found strange figures, still as statues. But none was the sleeping Princess the old man had spoken of. Just as the Prince was about to give up, he came at last to the room at the top of the narrow stairway.

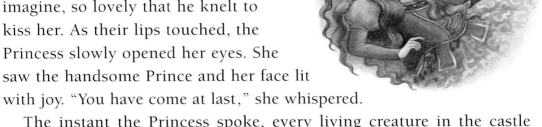

When he opened the door, he stared in awe. On the bed lay the Princess, still deep in her enchanted sleep. She was lovelier than the Prince had dared to imagine, so lovely that he knelt to kiss her. As their lips touched, the Princess slowly opened her eyes. She saw the handsome Prince and her face lit with joy. "You have come at last," she whispered.

The instant the Princess spoke, every living creature in the castle awakened, and the sound of laughter and revelry echoed throughout the halls.

Soon after, the Prince and Princess were married in a magnificent royal wedding. The guests rejoiced with the happy couple and everyone celebrated long into the night, so glad were they to be awake again after sleeping for one hundred years!

The Little Mermaid

Long ago, in the kingdom of the sea people, there lived a little mermaid. By day she and her sisters played among the coral reefs, collecting shells to braid into their long dark hair. The Little Mermaid sang as she played, and all who heard her were charmed by her beautiful voice. In the evening, the sisters gathered to hear the tales their grandmother told of the world above the sea. The Little Mermaid listened spellbound, wishing that she could see this wondrous world for herself.

"When you are fifteen years old, you may rise to the surface to see the human world," her grandmother promised.

On her fifteenth birthday, the Little Mermaid swam up eagerly. As she lifted her head out of the water, she saw a large ship floating in the glow of the setting sun. The Little Mermaid swam close enough to peek through one of the portholes.

Inside was a room filled with people feasting and celebrating. One stood out among the rest. He was a young prince, the handsomest creature she had ever seen.

The Little Mermaid was so entranced by the Prince, she scarcely noticed that the sea had begun to tremble beneath her. The sky grew black as night. Waves rocked and churned, tossing the ship about until suddenly, with a thunderous crack, it split in two. Everyone on board was flung into the raging water.

The Little Mermaid watched, horrified, as the Prince vanished beneath the waves. She dove again and again, searching until she found him. Then she rose to the surface and held his head up to the life-giving air. All through the night the Little Mermaid swam with the Prince in her arms, struggling against the waves that pushed them farther and farther out to sea.

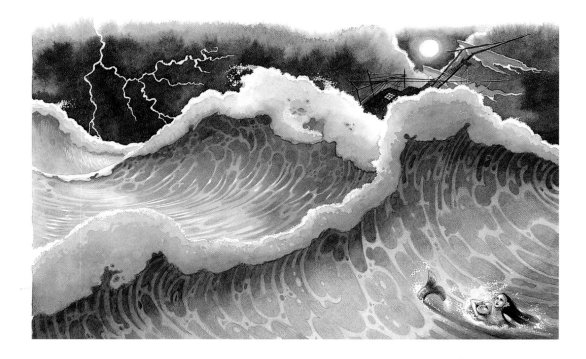

By morning the sea had calmed. Gathering her last bit of strength, the Little Mermaid managed to swim to the distant shore. She gently pushed the Prince onto the sand and touched her lips to his forehead. Then she hid behind a rock, watching to be sure that someone would find him.

Beyond the beach stood a tall white temple. A young girl came out and hurried toward the figure lying on the sand. As she knelt beside him, the Prince opened his eyes and smiled at her, for he believed that it was she who had saved his life.

How the Little Mermaid wished she could run to him and say, "I am the one who saved you!" But that was impossible for she had no legs, only a fish tail, which was useless in the Prince's world. Sorrowfully the Little Mermaid returned to the sea.

From then on, the Little Mermaid thought of no one but the Prince. She found the palace where he lived, with its broad steps leading down to the sea. In the evenings, the Little Mermaid swam closer to shore than her sisters had ever dared. She gazed at the Prince as he walked through the palace gardens. At times she sang to him, and the Prince would come to the foot of the steps, hoping to catch a glimpse of the girl who had such a beautiful voice. But she never let him see her.

Sometimes she watched the parties that took place on board his ship. The more the Little Mermaid saw of the Prince's world, the more she yearned to be part of it.

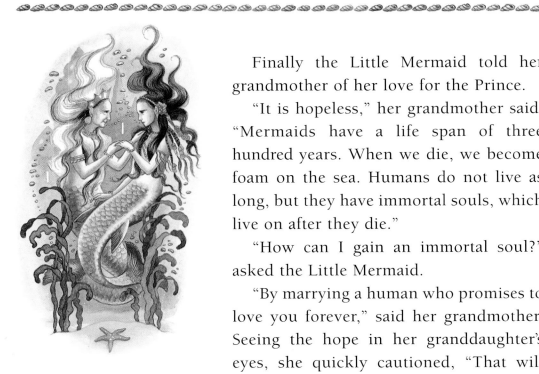

Finally the Little Mermaid told her grandmother of her love for the Prince.

"It is hopeless," her grandmother said. "Mermaids have a life span of three hundred years. When we die, we become foam on the sea. Humans do not live as long, but they have immortal souls, which live on after they die."

"How can I gain an immortal soul?" asked the Little Mermaid.

"By marrying a human who promises to love you forever," said her grandmother. Seeing the hope in her granddaughter's eyes, she quickly cautioned, "That will not happen. Humans scorn our beautiful tails because they think their clumsy legs are superior. You must forget this prince, for he will never marry a mermaid."

But the Little Mermaid could not forget the Prince. One day she set out for a secret place, in the darkest depths of the underwater world. Her heart pounded with fear as she swam through the murky water. Scaly creatures snatched at her with worm-like fingers. Below lay the rotting hulls of sunken ships and long-forgotten skeletons of sailors lost at sea. Finally the Little Mermaid reached the entrance to a gloomy cavern. There she came face to face with the ghastly Sea Witch.

"Foolish creature, I know why you have come," sneered the Sea Witch. Her eyes glittered with spite as she held out a vial of evil-smelling liquid. "Drink this and your tail will turn into legs. But be warned! Every step you take will bring pain, as if a fiery sword were being thrust into your feet. And I warn you of this as well: You must not fail to win the Prince's love. If he should marry another, on the morning after his wedding your life will end. You will become nothing more than foam on the sea."

The Little Mermaid reached for the vial, but the Sea Witch snatched it back. "Did you think I would let you have this for nothing?" she cackled. "In return you must give me your beautiful voice and remain silent forever."

"I will do it," said the Little Mermaid, and she took the vial. Then she swam back to have one last look at the sea kingdom, knowing that once she drank the magic potion, she could never return.

On the steps of the Prince's palace, the Little Mermaid put the vial to her lips. The moment she drank the bitter potion, such agonizing pain surged through her body that she fainted. When she opened her eyes again, her beautiful tail was gone. In its place were two human legs. The Little Mermaid looked up. The Prince was kneeling at her side. "Where did you come from?" he asked. The Little Mermaid tried to answer, but not a sound came from her lips.

The Prince took the Little Mermaid to live at his palace. From that day on, she knew both sorrow and joy. Her beautiful voice was gone, and every step she took brought almost unbearable pain. But she was with her beloved Prince, so she bore it bravely.

The Prince grew fond of his silent companion and told her all his secrets. He often talked about the beautiful girl who had saved him from drowning. "I see her face in my dreams," he said. "It is she alone whom I love, yet I fear I will never see her again."

"I am the one who saved you," the Little Mermaid longed to cry out, but she was locked in a world of silence.

Because the Prince loved only the girl he saw in his dreams, he refused to marry anyone else. Finally his parents took matters into their own hands and arranged a marriage for him. The Prince insisted that the Little Mermaid accompany the royal family as they sailed to the far-off city where the wedding would take place. When they arrived, the Prince saw his bride for the first time.

"It is you!" he cried with joy and amazement. Indeed, the girl standing before him was the very girl he believed had saved his life.

The wedding took place the next day. With a heavy heart, the Little Mermaid watched as the Prince and his bride embraced. It was then that she remembered the Sea Witch's second warning. Now she must give up not only the Prince but her life as well.

That evening, back on board the ship, the Prince and his bride retired to their bedchamber. The Little Mermaid stood on the deck alone, looking out at the sea. Suddenly, in the moon's silver path, the waves parted and her sisters appeared. Their faces bobbed above the surface, pale and fragile as water lilies, for their long hair was now cut short. They swam to the side of the ship, and the eldest held up a silver dagger.

"Sister, we bargained this from the Sea Witch in exchange for our hair," she called. "The Sea Witch said that you may still save yourself. A few drops of the Prince's blood on your feet will change your legs back into a mermaid's tail, and you can return to our home in the sea."

She tossed the dagger up to her sister. The Little Mermaid caught it. She tiptoed to the Prince's bedchamber and pulled back the curtain. The Prince and his bride lay sleeping, their arms entwined. With a trembling hand, the Little Mermaid raised the dagger.

But she could not do the deed. Although she yearned to join her sisters, the Little Mermaid could not harm the Prince. She ran from the bedchamber and flung the dagger overboard. It sank, leaving behind a crimson froth.

As the first glimmer of sunrise appeared on the horizon, the Little Mermaid dove into the sea. "Now I must die, just as the Sea Witch warned," she thought. But then, as her body began to dissolve into sea foam, she looked up and saw a beautiful sight. Hundreds of transparent creatures were floating in the air above her.

"Come with us to the spirit world," they called.

"Who are you?" asked the Little Mermaid.

"We are the daughters of the air," they replied. "Like you, we do not have immortal souls. But we may earn them if, for three hundred years, we do good deeds for others. You endured great pain and hardship to win the Prince's love, and you would not harm him to save yourself. In reward for such goodness, you need not die. You may become one of us and earn an immortal soul."

The Little Mermaid took one last look at the ship. "If I cannot live with my Prince in the human world, then I must find happiness elsewhere," she thought. She lifted her eyes to the sun. Its brilliant rays seemed to welcome her as she rose to join the daughters of the air.

Beauty and the Beast

There was once a rich merchant who lived in luxury with his three lovely daughters. The youngest was called Beauty, and she was the fairest by far.

The merchant took great pleasure in giving his daughters everything their hearts desired. The two eldest demanded the finest clothes, the richest furs and the most costly jewels. They took everything their father gave with scarcely a word of thanks in return. Beauty asked only for her father's love, and this he gave more gladly than any worldly goods.

One day word came that the merchant's fleet of ships had been lost at sea. With his wealth now gone, the merchant had no choice but to sell his grand home and all his possessions to pay his debts. Soon after, the family moved to a small farm in the country. Beauty made the best of it, for she knew that her father was heartbroken. While her sisters moped about, complaining bitterly of their reduced circumstances, Beauty helped run the farm as best she could.

Then, to everyone's relief, came the news that one of the merchant's ships had arrived back in port. "We may be rich again!" the merchant cried, hugging his daughters joyfully. "I must go at once and see to business. What presents shall I bring you?"

The older girls clamored for dresses and wigs and costly baubles of all kinds. How they snickered and sneered when Beauty asked only for a single red rose.

The merchant saddled his horse and rode swiftly to the dockyard. He arrived with high hopes only to find that the ship, ransacked by thieves and damaged beyond repair, was now worthless. He had no choice but to turn back home empty-handed.

As if he weren't burdened with troubles enough, the merchant was soon caught in a fierce blizzard that seemed to blow up from nowhere. Snow swirled around him in such wild gusts that he could no longer see the path. He lost his way and rode deeper and deeper into a vast forest.

He had almost given up hope of surviving when a gleam of light caught his eye. In that instant, the biting wind calmed and the blowing snow turned to gently falling flakes. The merchant could now see that the light came from a magnificent castle towering above the trees ahead. With a thankful cry, he urged his weary horse onward.

When he reached the courtyard, the glow of lantern light led the merchant to a stable. Inside he found fresh hay and water. He fed his horse, drew his heavy cloak around him and made his way to the castle.

The huge oak doors stood open as if in welcome. The merchant walked in, hoping to find someone whom he could ask for a night's lodging. But there was not a soul in sight. He wandered from room to room, gazing in wonder at the elegant surroundings.

Finally the merchant came to the great dining hall. There he found a table laden with a tempting feast, yet this room was as silent and deserted as the rest. Overcome by hunger, the merchant sat down and ate until he could eat no more. Exhausted, he stumbled into the nearest bedchamber and fell asleep.

When he woke, sunlight was streaming through the casement windows. On a chair next to the bed lay a fresh set of clothes. A plate of biscuits and a pot of hot chocolate stood on a nearby table. The merchant dressed and ate quickly. Then he hurried to the stable to saddle his horse.

As he entered the courtyard he stopped and stared. Yet another wonder greeted his eyes. Beyond the stables was a glorious rose garden. At the edge was a bush covered with blood-red blossoms. "I must pick just one for Beauty," the merchant decided.

The instant he plucked the rose, a dreadful roar split the stillness and a hideous beast appeared before him.

"Ungrateful wretch!" thundered the Beast. "I gave you food and shelter and you thank me by stealing the thing I love most. For this you will pay with your life!"

Terrified, the merchant begged forgiveness. "I took the rose for my daughter, Beauty. In all the world, there is nothing I love more than her."

"Since you have taken what I love, you must give me what you love," growled the Beast. "Go now and send Beauty to me within three months' time. She will live here and come to no harm. Otherwise you must promise to return yourself and accept your punishment."

The merchant gave a silent nod of agreement. He had no intention of sending his beloved Beauty to the Beast. Instead he resolved to go home and bid farewell to his daughters, then return to the castle himself to pay his debt to the Beast.

"You may go," said the Beast, "but if you want me to spare your life, do not forget your promise."

When the merchant arrived home, the two eldest daughters demanded their presents. "All I could bring back is this rose," their father said. The two sisters glowered as he handed it to Beauty. Then he told his daughters all that had happened, but he did not mention the promise he had made to the Beast.

As the weeks passed, Beauty saw that her father was becoming more and more distraught. She pleaded with him to tell her what was the matter. Finally he revealed his terrible secret.

"Oh, Beauty, what have I done?" he cried.

"Don't worry, father," said Beauty. "I will gladly go in your place, for you have suffered enough." And so it was that Beauty went to live at the Beast's castle.

When she first saw the Beast, Beauty gasped in alarm at his hideous appearance. But he spoke to her so kindly that she soon overcame her fear. "You are mistress here," he told her. "You may go wherever you wish."

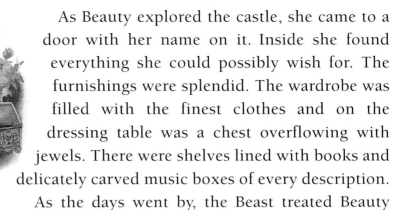

As Beauty explored the castle, she came to a door with her name on it. Inside she found everything she could possibly wish for. The furnishings were splendid. The wardrobe was filled with the finest clothes and on the dressing table was a chest overflowing with jewels. There were shelves lined with books and delicately carved music boxes of every description.

As the days went by, the Beast treated Beauty with every kindness and courtesy. Soon she began to look forward to the time they spent together. They often walked through the gardens, admiring the roses the Beast tended with such care. While Beauty dined, the Beast sat by her side, anxious to know that everything was exactly as she liked it. In the evenings he read to her. And each night before she went to bed, the Beast asked the same question: "Beauty, will you marry me?"

Beauty always replied, "No, Beast, I cannot," but her heart ached to see the sadness her words caused him.

This was not her only sorrow, for she also missed her father dearly. One evening the Beast gave Beauty a gold mirror. "Look into it and you will see whoever is in your thoughts," he said. When she did, Beauty saw her father lying ill in bed.

"Please let me go to him," she pleaded.

The Beast hesitated. Then he said gently, "You may go, Beauty, but you must return in eight days. If you do not, I shall die of sorrow."

When Beauty gave her promise, the Beast put a gold ring on her finger. "A twist of this ring will take you wherever you want to go," he said. "Do not forget your promise to me."

No sooner had Beauty wished herself home than she was there. How she and her father rejoiced at the sight of one another! Though her sisters pretended to be happy to see Beauty, their hearts held nothing but envy for the beautiful clothes and jewels the Beast had given her.

All too soon, the eighth day arrived. Beauty told her father and sisters of her promise to return to the Beast. Now her jealous sisters saw a way to end Beauty's good fortune.

"How can you think of leaving Father?" demanded the eldest.

"He will die of sorrow," said the other. "And we will die of loneliness without you."

Beauty knew nothing of trickery and deceit. She believed her sisters and so she stayed on. Yet as the days passed, Beauty found herself thinking more and more often of the Beast. One day she looked into the gold mirror and a chill pierced her heart. Beside the rose garden lay the Beast, still as stone.

In that moment, Beauty realized that she had come to love the Beast with all her heart. She twisted the ring and was instantly at his side.

"Do not die, my beloved," she pleaded, cradling his head in her arms.

The Beast looked up at her. "You came back to me," he said.

"I have kept my promise," Beauty replied, "for I have grown to love you with all my heart."

The words were hardly out of her mouth when, before her eyes, the hideous Beast turned into a handsome prince.

"Years ago an evil spell changed me into a Beast," explained the Prince. "Now, at last, the enchantment has been broken because you learned to love me as I was." His eyes shone with adoration. "Beauty, will you marry me?" he asked.

"Yes, I will," Beauty replied.

Two months later, with her father at her side and her sisters sulking in the background, Beauty and the Prince were married in the castle's glorious rose garden. Together they found happiness and contentment that would last for the rest of their lives.